Another Study of Woman

Honore de Balzac

Translator: Ellen Marriage and
Clara Bell

Contents

ANOTHER STUDY
OF WOMAN

BY

Honore de Balzac

Translator: Ellen Marriage and Clara Bell

ANOTHER STUDY OF WOMAN

BY

HONORE DE BALZAC

Translated by

Ellen Marriage and Clara Bell

DEDICATION

To Leon Gozlan as a Token of Literary Good-fellowship.

ANOTHER STUDY OF WOMAN

At Paris there are almost always two separate parties going on at every ball and rout. First, an official party, composed of the persons invited, a fashionable and much-bored circle. Each one grimaces for his neighbor's eye; most of the younger women are there for one person only; when each woman has assured herself that for that one she is the handsomest woman in the room, and that the opinion is perhaps shared by a few others, a few insignificant phrases are exchanged, as: "Do you think of going away soon to La Crampade?" "How well Madame de Portenduere sang!" "Who is that little woman with such a load of diamonds?" Or, after firing off some smart epigrams, which give transient pleasure, and leave wounds that rankle long, the groups thin out, the mere lookers on go away, and the waxlights burn down to the sconces.

The mistress of the house then waylays a few artists, amusing people or intimate friends, saying, "Do not go yet; we will have a snug little supper." These collect in some small room. The second, the real party, now begins; a party where, as of old, every one can hear what is said, conversation is general, each one is bound to be witty and to contribute to the amusement of all. Everything is made to tell, honest laughter takes the place of the gloom which in company saddens the prettiest faces. In short, where the rout ends pleasure begins.

The Rout, a cold display of luxury, a review of self-conceits in full dress, is one of those English inventions which tend to ***mechanize*** other nations. England seems bent on seeing the whole world as dull as itself, and dull in the same way. So this second party is, in some French houses, a happy protest on the part of the old spirit of our light-hearted people. Only, unfortunately, so few houses protest; and the reason is a simple one. If we no longer have many suppers nowadays, it is because never, under any rule, have there been fewer men placed, established, and successful than under the reign of Louis Philippe, when the Revolution began again, lawfully. Everybody is on the march some whither, or trotting at the heels of Fortune. Time has become the costliest commodity, so no one can afford the lavish extravagance of going home to-morrow morning and getting up late. Hence, there is no second soiree now but at the houses of women rich enough to entertain, and since July 1830 such women may be counted in Paris.

In spite of the covert opposition of the Faubourg Saint-Germain, two or three women, among them Madame d'Espard and Mademoiselle des Touches, have not chosen to give up the share of influence they exercised in Paris, and have not closed their houses.

The salon of Mademoiselle des Touches is noted in Paris as being the last refuge where the old French wit has found a home, with its reserved depths, its myriad subtle byways, and its exquisite politeness. You will there still find grace of manner notwithstanding the conventionalities of courtesy, perfect freedom of talk notwith-standing the reserve which is natural to persons of breeding, and, above all, a liberal flow of ideas. No one there thinks of keeping his thought for a play; and no one regards a story as material for a book. In short, the hideous skeleton of literature at bay never stalks there, on the prowl for a clever sally or an interesting subject.

The memory of one of these evenings especially dwells with me, less by reason of a confidence in which the illustrious de Marsay opened up one of the deepest recesses of woman's heart, than on account of the reflections to which his narrative gave rise, as to the changes that have taken place in the French woman since the fateful revolution of July.

On that evening chance had brought together several persons, whose indisputable merits have won them European reputations. This is not a piece of flattery addressed to France, for there were a good many foreigners present. And, indeed, the men who most shone were not the most famous. Ingenious repartee, acute remarks, admirable banter, pictures sketched with brilliant precision, all sparkled and flowed without elaboration, were poured out without disdain, but without effort, and were exquisitely expressed and delicately appreciated. The men of the world especially were conspicuous for their really artistic grace and spirit.

Elsewhere in Europe you will find elegant manners, cordiality, genial fellowship, and knowledge; but only in Paris, in this drawing-room, and those to which I have alluded, does the particular wit abound which gives an agreeable and changeful unity to all these social qualities, an indescribable river-like flow which makes this profusion of ideas, of definitions, of anecdotes, of historical incidents, meander with ease. Paris, the capital of taste, alone possesses the science which makes conversation a tourney in which each type of wit is condensed into a shaft, each speaker utters his phrase and casts his experience in a word, in which every one finds amusement, relaxation, and exercise. Here, then, alone, will you exchange ideas; here you need not, like the dolphin in the fable, carry a monkey on your shoulders; here you will be understood, and will not risk staking your gold pieces against base metal.

Here, again, secrets neatly betrayed, and talk, light or deep, play and eddy, changing their aspect and hue at every phrase. Eager criticism and crisp anecdotes lead on from one to the next. All eyes are listening, a gesture asks a question, and an expressive look gives the answer. In short, and in a word, everything is wit and mind.

The phenomenon of speech, which, when duly studied and well handled, is the power of the actor and the story-teller, had never so completely bewitched me. Nor was I alone under the influence of its spell; we all spent a delightful evening. The conversation had drifted into anecdote, and brought out in its rushing course some curious confessions, several portraits, and a thousand follies, which make this enchanting improvisation impossible to record; still, by setting these things down in all their natural freshness and abruptness, their elusive divarications, you may perhaps feel the charm of a real French evening, taken at the moment when the most engaging familiarity makes each one forget his own interests, his personal conceit, or, if you like, his pretensions.

At about two in the morning, as supper ended, no one was left sitting round the table but intimate friends, proved by intercourse of fifteen years, and some persons of great taste and good breeding, who knew the world. By tacit agreement, perfectly carried out, at supper every one renounced his pretensions to importance. Perfect equality set the tone. But indeed there was no one present who was not very proud of being himself.

Mademoiselle des Touches always insists on her guests remaining at table till they leave, having frequently remarked the change which a move produces in the spirit of a party. Between the dining-room and the drawing-room the charm is destroyed. According to Sterne, the ideas of an author after shaving are different from those he had before. If Sterne is right, may it not be boldly asserted that the frame of mind of a party at table is not the same as that of the same persons returned to the drawing-room? The atmosphere is not heady, the eye no longer contemplates the brilliant disorder of the dessert, lost are the happy effects of that laxness of mood, that benevolence which comes over us while we remain in the humor peculiar to the well-filled man, settled comfortably on one of the springy chairs which are made in these days. Perhaps we are not more ready to talk face to face with the dessert and in the society of good wine, during the delightful interval when every one may sit with an elbow on the table and his head resting on his hand. Not only does every one like to talk then, but also to listen. Digestion, which is almost always attent, is loquacious or silent, as characters differ. Then every one finds his opportunity.

Was not this preamble necessary to make you know the charm of the narrative, by which a celebrated man, now dead, depicted the innocent jesuistry of women, painting it with the subtlety peculiar to persons who have seen much of the world, and which makes statesmen such delightful storytellers when, like Prince Talleyrand and Prince Metternich, they vouchsafe to tell a story?

De Marsay, prime minister for some six months, had already given proofs of superior capabilities. Those who had known him long were not indeed surprised to see him display all the talents and various aptitudes of a statesman; still it might yet be a question whether he would prove to be a solid politician, or had merely been moulded in the fire of circumstance. This question had just been asked by a man whom he had made a prefet, a man of wit and observation, who had for a long time been a journalist, and who admired de Marsay without infusing into his admiration that dash of acrid criticism by which, in Paris, one superior man excuses himself from admiring another.

"Was there ever," said he, "in your former life, any event, any thought or wish which told you what your vocation was?" asked Emile Blondet; "for we all, like Newton, have our apple, which falls and leads us to the spot where our faculties develop----"

"Yes," said de Marsay; "I will tell you about it."

Pretty women, political dandies, artists, old men, de Marsay's intimate friends,--all settled themselves comfortably, each in his favorite attitude, to look at the Minister. Need it be said that the servants had left, that the doors were shut, and the curtains drawn over them? The silence was so complete that the murmurs of the coachmen's voices could be heard from the courtyard, and the pawing and champing made by horses when asking to be taken back to their stable.

"The statesman, my friends, exists by one single quality," said the Minister, playing with his gold and mother-of-pearl dessert knife. "To wit: the power of always being master of himself; of profiting more or less, under all circumstances, by every event, however fortuitous; in short, of having within himself a cold and disinterested other self, who looks on as a spectator at all the changes of life, noting our passions and our sentiments, and whispering to us in every case the judgment of a sort of moral ready-reckoner."

"That explains why a statesman is so rare a thing in France," said old Lord Dudley.

"From a sentimental point of view, this is horrible," the Minister went on. "Hence, when such a phenomenon is seen in a young man --Richelieu, who, when warned overnight by a letter of Concini's peril, slept till midday, when his benefactor was killed at ten o'clock--or say Pitt, or Napoleon, he was a monster. I became such a monster at a very early age, thanks to a woman."

"I fancied," said Madame de Montcornet with a smile, "that more politicians were undone by us than we could make."

"The monster of which I speak is a monster just because he withstands you," replied de Marsay, with a little ironical bow.

"If this is a love-story," the Baronne de Nucingen interposed, "I request that it may not be interrupted by any reflections."

"Reflection is so antipathetic to it!" cried Joseph Bridau.

"I was seventeen," de Marsay went on; "the Restoration was being consolidated; my old friends know how impetuous and fervid I was then. I was in love for the first time, and I was--I may say so now--one of the handsomest young fellows in Paris. I had youth and good looks, two advantages due to good fortune, but of which we are all as proud as of a conquest. I must be silent as to the rest.--Like all youths, I was in love with a woman six years older than myself. No one of you here," said he, looking carefully round the table, "can suspect her name or recognize her. Ronquerolles alone, at the time, ever guessed my secret. He had kept it well, but I should have feared his smile. However, he is gone," said the Minister, looking round.

"He would not stay to supper," said Madame de Nucingen.

"For six months, possessed by my passion," de Marsay went on, "but incapable of suspecting that it had overmastered me, I had abandoned myself to that rapturous idolatry which is at once the triumph and the frail joy of the young. I treasured *her* old gloves; I drank an infusion of the flowers *she* had worn; I got out of bed at night to go and gaze at *her* window. All my blood rushed to my heart when I inhaled the perfume she used. I was miles away from knowing that woman is a stove with a marble casing."

"Oh! spare us your terrible verdicts," cried Madame de Montcornet with a smile.

"I believe I should have crushed with my scorn the philosopher who first uttered this terrible but profoundly true thought," said de Marsay. "You are all far too keen-sighted for me to say any more on that point. These few words will remind you of your own follies.

"A great lady if ever there was one, a widow without children--oh! all was perfect--my idol would shut herself up to mark my linen with her hair; in short, she responded to my madness by her own. And how can we fail to believe in passion when it has the guarantee of madness?

"We each devoted all our minds to concealing a love so perfect and so beautiful from the eyes of the world; and we succeeded. And what charm we found in our escapades! Of her I will say nothing. She was perfection then, and to this day is considered one of the most beautiful women in Paris; but at that time a man would have endured death to win one of her glances. She had been left with an amount of fortune sufficient for a woman who had loved and was adored; but the Restoration, to which she owed renewed lustre, made it seem inadequate in comparison with her name. In my position I was so fatuous as never to dream of a suspicion. Though my jealousy would have been of a hundred and twenty Othello-power, that terrible passion slumbered in me as gold in the nugget. I would have ordered my servant to thrash me if I had been so base as ever to doubt the purity of that angel--so fragile and so strong, so fair, so artless, pure, spotless, and whose blue eyes allowed my gaze to sound it to the very depths of her heart with adorable submissiveness. Never was there the slightest hesitancy in her attitude, her look, or word; always white and fresh, and ready for the Beloved like the Oriental Lily of the 'Song of Songs!' Ah! my friends!" sadly exclaimed the Minister, grown young again, "a man must hit his head very hard on the marble to dispel that poem!"

This cry of nature, finding an echo in the listeners, spurred the curiosity he had excited in them with so much skill.

"Every morning, riding Sultan--the fine horse you sent me from England," de Marsay went on, addressing Lord Dudley, "I rode past her open carriage, the horses' pace being intentionally reduced to a walk, and read the order of the day signaled to me by the flowers of her bouquet in case we were unable to exchange a few words. Though we saw each other almost every evening in society, and she wrote to me every day, to deceive the curious and mislead the observant we had adopted a scheme of conduct: never to look at each other; to avoid meeting; to speak ill of each other. Self-admiration, swagger, or playing the disdained swain,--all these old manoeuvres are not to compare on either part with a false passion professed for an indifferent person and an air of indifference towards the true idol. If two lovers will only play that game, the world will always be deceived; but then they must be very secure of each other.

"Her stalking-horse was a man in high favor, a courtier, cold and sanctimonious, whom she never received at her own house. This little comedy was performed for the benefit of simpletons and drawing-room circles, who laughed at it.

Marriage was never spoken of between us; six years' difference of age might give her pause; she knew nothing of my fortune, of which, on principle, I have always kept the secret. I, on my part, fascinated by her wit and manners, by the extent of her knowledge and her experience of the world, would have married her without a thought. At the same time, her reserve charmed me. If she had been the first to speak of marriage in a certain tone, I might perhaps have noted it as vulgar in that accomplished soul.

"Six months, full and perfect--a diamond of the purest water! That has been my portion of love in this base world.

"One morning, attacked by the feverish stiffness which marks the beginning of a cold, I wrote her a line to put off one of those secret festivals which are buried under the roofs of Paris like pearls in the sea. No sooner was the letter sent than re-morse seized me: she will not believe that I am ill! thought I. She was wont to affect jealousy and suspiciousness.--When jealousy is genuine," said de Marsay, interrupt-ing himself, "it is the visible sign of an unique passion."

"Why?" asked the Princesse de Cadignan eagerly.

"Unique and true love," said de Marsay, "produces a sort of corporeal apathy attuned to the contemplation into which one falls. Then the mind complicates ev-erything; it works on itself, pictures its fancies, turns them into reality and torment; and such jealousy is as delightful as it is distressing."

A foreign minister smiled as, by the light of memory, he felt the truth of this remark.

"Besides," de Marsay went on, "I said to myself, why miss a happy hour? Was it not better to go, even though feverish? And, then, if she learns that I am ill, I believe her capable of hurrying here and compromising herself. I made an effort; I wrote a second letter, and carried it myself, for my confidential servant was now gone. The river lay between us. I had to cross Paris; but at last, within a suitable distance of her house, I caught sight of a messenger; I charged him to have the note sent up to her at once, and I had the happy idea of driving past her door in a hack-ney cab to see whether she might not by chance receive the two letters together. At the moment when I arrived it was two o'clock; the great gate opened to admit a carriage. Whose? --That of the stalking-horse!

"It is fifteen years since--well, even while I tell the tale, I, the exhausted orator, the Minister dried up by the friction of public business, I still feel a surging in my heart and the hot blood about my diaphragm. At the end of an hour I passed once more; the carriage was still in the courtyard! My note no doubt was in the porter's hands. At last, at half-past three, the carriage drove out. I could observe my rival's expression; he was grave, and did not smile; but he was in love, and no doubt there was business in hand.

"I went to keep my appointment; the queen of my heart met me; I saw her calm, pure, serene. And here I must confess that I have always thought that Othello was not only stupid, but showed very bad taste. Only a man who is half a Negro could behave so: indeed Shakespeare felt this when he called his play 'The Moor of Venice.' The sight of the woman we love is such a balm to the heart that it must dispel anguish, doubt, and sorrow. All my rage vanished. I could smile again. Hence this cheerfulness, which at my age now would be the most atrocious dissimulation, was the result of my youth and my love. My jealousy once buried, I had the power of observation. My ailing condition was evident; the horrible doubts that had fermented in me increased it. At last I found an opening for putting in these words: 'You have had no one with you this morning?' making a pretext of the uneasiness I had felt in the fear lest she should have disposed of her time after receiving my first note.--'Ah!' she exclaimed, 'only a man could have such ideas! As if I could think of anything but your suffering. Till the moment when I received your second note I could think only of how I could contrive to see you.'--'And you were alone?'--'Alone,' said she, looking at me with a face of innocence so perfect that it must have been his distrust of such a look as that which made the Moor kill Desdemona. As she lived alone in the house, the word was a fearful lie. One single lie destroys the absolute confidence which to some souls is the very foundation of happiness.

"To explain to you what passed in me at that moment it must be assumed that we have an internal self of which the exterior *I* is but the husk; that this self, as brilliant as light, is as fragile as a shade --well, that beautiful self was in me thenceforth for ever shrouded in crape. Yes; I felt a cold and fleshless hand cast over me the winding-sheet of experience, dooming me to the eternal mourning into which the first betrayal plunges the soul. As I cast my eyes down that she might not observe my dizziness, this proud thought somewhat restored my strength: 'If she is deceiving you, she is unworthy of you!'

"I ascribed my sudden reddening and the tears which started to my eyes to an attack of pain, and the sweet creature insisted on driving me home with the blinds of the cab drawn. On the way she was full of a solicitude and tenderness that might have deceived the Moor of Venice whom I have taken as a standard of comparison. Indeed, if that great child were to hesitate two seconds longer, every intelligent spectator feels that he would ask Desdemona's forgiveness. Thus, killing the woman is the act of a boy.--She wept as we parted, so much was she distressed at being unable to nurse me herself. She wished she were my valet, in whose happiness she found a cause of envy, and all this was as elegantly expressed, oh! as Clarissa might have written in her happiness. There is always a precious ape in the prettiest and most angelic woman!"

At these words all the women looked down, as if hurt by this brutal truth so brutally stated.

"I will say nothing of the night, nor of the week I spent," de Marsay went on. "I discovered that I was a statesman."

It was so well said that we all uttered an admiring exclamation.

"As I thought over the really cruel vengeance to be taken on a woman," said de Marsay, continuing his story, "with infernal ingenuity--for, as we had loved each other, some terrible and irreparable revenges were possible--I despised myself, I felt how common I was, I insensibly formulated a horrible code--that of Indulgence. In taking vengeance on a woman, do we not in fact admit that there is but one for us, that we cannot do without her? And, then, is revenge the way to win her back? If she is not indispensable, if there are other women in the world, why not grant her the right to change which we assume?

"This, of course, applies only to passion; in any other sense it would be socially wrong. Nothing more clearly proves the necessity for indissoluble marriage than the instability of passion. The two sexes must be chained up, like wild beasts as they are, by inevitable law, deaf and mute. Eliminate revenge, and infidelity in love is nothing. Those who believe that for them there is but one woman in the world must be in favor of vengeance, and then there is but one form of it --that of Othello.

"Mine was different."

The words produced in each of us the imperceptible movement which newspaper writers represent in Parliamentary reports by the words: ***great sensation***.

"Cured of my cold, and of my pure, absolute, divine love, I flung myself into an adventure, of which the heroine was charming, and of a style of beauty utterly opposed to that of my deceiving angel. I took care not to quarrel with this clever woman, who was so good an actress, for I doubt whether true love can give such gracious delights as those lavished by such a dexterous fraud. Such refined hypocrisy is as good as virtue.--I am not speaking to you Englishwomen, my lady," said the Minister, suavely, addressing Lady Barimore, Lord Dudley's daughter. "I tried to be the same lover.

"I wished to have some of my hair worked up for my new angel, and I went to a skilled artist who at that time dwelt in the Rue Boucher. The man had a monopoly of capillary keepsakes, and I mention his address for the benefit of those who have not much hair; he has plenty of every kind and every color. After I had explained my order, he showed me his work. I then saw achievements of patience surpassing those which the story books ascribe to fairies, or which are executed by prisoners. He brought me up to date as to the caprices and fashions governing the use of hair. 'For the last year,' said he, 'there has been a rage for marking linen with hair; happily I had a fine collection of hair and skilled needlewomen,'--on hearing this a suspicion flashed upon me; I took out my handkerchief and said, 'So this was done in your shop, with false hair?'--He looked at the handkerchief, and said, 'Ay! that lady was very particular, she insisted on verifying the tint of the hair. My wife herself marked those handkerchiefs. You have there, sir, one of the finest pieces of work we have ever executed.' Before this last ray of light I might have believed something--might have taken a woman's word. I left the shop still having faith in pleasure, but where love was concerned I was as atheistical as a mathematician.

"Two months later I was sitting by the side of the ethereal being in her boudoir, on her sofa; I was holding one of her hands--they were very beautiful--and we scaled the Alps of sentiment, culling their sweetest flowers, and pulling off the daisy-petals; there is always a moment when one pulls daisies to pieces, even if it is in a drawing-room and there are no daisies. At the intensest moment of tenderness, and when we are most in love, love is so well aware of its own short duration that we are irresistibly urged to ask, 'Do you love me? Will you love me always?' I seized the elegiac moment, so warm, so flowery, so full-blown, to lead her to tell her most delightful lies, in the enchanting language of love. Charlotte displayed her choicest allurements: She could not live without me; I was to her the only man in the world; she feared to weary me, because my presence bereft her of all her wits; with me, all her faculties were lost in love; she was indeed too tender to escape alarms; for the last six months she had been seeking some way to bind me to her eternally, and God alone knew that secret; in short, I was her god!"

The women who heard de Marsay seemed offended by seeing themselves so well acted, for he seconded the words by airs, and sidelong attitudes, and mincing grimaces which were quite illusory.

"At the very moment when I might have believed these adorable falsehoods, as I still held her right hand in mine, I said to her, 'When are you to marry the Duke?'

"The thrust was so direct, my gaze met hers so boldly, and her hand lay so tightly in mine, that her start, slight as it was, could not be disguised; her eyes fell before mine, and a faint blush colored her cheeks.--'The Duke! What do you mean?' she said, affecting great astonishment.--'I know everything,' replied I; 'and in my opinion, you should delay no longer; he is rich; he is a duke; but he is more than devout, he is religious! I am sure, therefore, that you have been faithful to me, thanks to his scruples. You cannot imagine how urgently necessary it is that you should compromise him with himself and with God; short of that you will never bring him to the point.' --'Is this a dream?' said she, pushing her hair from her forehead, fifteen years before Malibran, with the gesture which Malibran has made so famous.--'Come, do not be childish, my angel,' said I, trying to take her hands; but she folded them before her with a little prudish and indignant mein.--'Marry him, you have my permission,' said I, replying to this gesture by using the formal ***vous*** instead of ***tu***. 'Nay, better, I beg you to do so.'--'But,' cried she, falling at my knees, 'there is some horrible mistake; I love no one in the world but you; you may demand any proofs you please.'--'Rise, my dear,' said I, 'and do me the honor of being truthful.'--'As before God.'--'Do you doubt my love?'--'No.'--'Nor my fidelity?'--'No.'--'Well, I have committed the greatest crime,' I went on. 'I have doubted your love and your fidelity. Between two intoxications I looked calmly about me.'--'Calmly!' sighed she. 'That is enough, Henri; you no longer love me.'

"She had at once found, you perceive, a loophole for escape. In scenes like these an adverb is dangerous. But, happily, curiosity made her add: 'And what did you see?

Have I ever spoken of the Duke excepting in public? Have you detected in my eyes----?'--'No,' said I, 'but in his. And you have eight times made me go to Saint-Thomas d'Aquin to see you listening to the same mass as he.'--'Ah!' she exclaimed, 'then I have made you jealous!'--Oh! I only wish I could be!' said I, admiring the pliancy of her quick intelligence, and these acrobatic feats which can only be successful in the eyes of the blind. 'But by dint of going to church I have become very incredulous. On the day of my first cold, and your first treachery, when you thought I was in bed, you received the Duke, and you told me you had seen no one.'--'Do you know that your conduct is infamous?'--'In what respect? I consider your marriage to the Duke an excellent arrangement; he gives you a great name, the only rank that suits you, a brilliant and distinguished position. You will be one of the queens of Paris. I should be doing you a wrong if I placed any obstacle in the way of this prospect, this distinguished life, this splendid alliance. Ah! Charlotte, some day you will do me justice by discovering how unlike my character is to that of other young men. You would have been compelled to deceive me; yes, you would have found it very difficult to break with me, for he watches you. It is time that we should part, for the Duke is rigidly virtuous. You must turn prude; I advise you to do so. The Duke is vain; he will be proud of his wife.'--'Oh!' cried she, bursting into tears, 'Henri, if only you had spoken! Yes, if you had chosen'--it was I who was to blame, you understand--'we would have gone to live all our days in a corner, married, happy, and defied the world.'--'Well, it is too late now,' said I, kissing her hands, and putting on a victimized air.--'Good God! But I can undo it all!' said she.--'No, you have gone too far with the Duke. I ought indeed to go a journey to part us more effectually. We should both have reason to fear our own affection----'--'Henri, do you think the Duke has any suspicions?' I was still 'Henri,' but the *tu* was lost for ever.--'I do not think so,' I replied, assuming the manner of a friend; 'but be as devout as possible, reconcile yourself to God, for the Duke waits for proofs; he hesitates, you must bring him to the point.'

"She rose, and walked twice round the boudoir in real or affected agitation; then she no doubt found an attitude and a look beseeming the new state of affairs, for she stopped in front of me, held out her hand, and said in a voice broken by emotion, 'Well, Henri, you are loyal, noble, and a charming man; I shall never forget you.'

"These were admirable tactics. She was bewitching in this transition of feeling, indispensable to the situation in which she wished to place herself in regard to me. I fell into the attitude, the manners, and the look of a man so deeply distressed, that I saw her too newly assumed dignity giving way; she looked at me, took my hand, drew me along almost, threw me on the sofa, but quite gently, and said after a moment's silence, 'I am dreadfully unhappy, my dear fellow. Do you love me?'--'Oh! yes.'--'Well, then, what will become of you?'"

At this point the women all looked at each other.

"Though I can still suffer when I recall her perfidy, I still laugh at her expression of entire conviction and sweet satisfaction that I must die, or at any rate sink into perpetual melancholy," de Marsay went on. "Oh! do not laugh yet!" he said to his listeners; "there is better to come. I looked at her very tenderly after a pause, and said to her, 'Yes, that is what I have been wondering.'--'Well, what will you do?' --'I asked myself that the day after my cold.'--'And----?' she asked with eager anxiety.--'And I have made advances to the little lady to whom I was supposed to be attached.'

"Charlotte started up from the sofa like a frightened doe, trembling like a leaf, gave me one of those looks in which women forgo all their dignity, all their modesty, their refinement, and even their grace, the sparkling glitter of a hunted viper's eye when driven into a corner, and said, 'And I have loved this man! I have struggled! I have----' On this last thought, which I leave you to guess, she made the most impressive pause I ever heard.--'Good God!' she cried, 'how unhappy are we women! we never can be loved. To you there is nothing serious in the purest feelings. But never mind; when you cheat us you still are our dupes!'--'I see that plainly,' said I, with a stricken air; 'you have far too much wit in your anger for your heart to suffer from it.'--This modest epigram increased her rage; she found some tears of vexation. 'You disgust me with the world and with life.' she said; 'you snatch away all my illusions; you deprave my heart.'

"She said to me all that I had a right to say to her, and with a simple effrontery, an artless audacity, which would certainly have nailed any man but me on the spot.--'What is to become of us poor women in a state of society such as Louis XVIII.'s charter made it?' --(Imagine how her words had run away with her.)--'Yes, indeed, we are born to suffer. In matters of passion we are always superior to you, and you are beneath all loyalty. There is no honesty in your hearts. To you love is a game in which you always cheat.'--'My dear,' said I, 'to take anything serious in society nowadays would be like making romantic love to an actress.'--'What a shameless betrayal! It was deliberately planned!'--'No, only a rational issue.'--'Good-bye, Monsieur de Marsay,' said she; 'you have deceived me horribly.' --'Surely,' I replied, taking up a submissive attitude, 'Madame la Duchesse will not remember Charlotte's grievances?'--'Certainly,' she answered bitterly.--'Then, in fact, you hate me?'--She bowed, and I said to myself, 'There is something still left!'

"The feeling she had when I parted from her allowed her to believe that she still had something to avenge. Well, my friends, I have carefully studied the lives of men who have had great success with women, but I do not believe that the Marechal de Richelieu, or Lauzun, or Louis de Valois ever effected a more judicious retreat at the first attempt. As to my mind and heart, they were cast in a mould then and there, once for all, and the power of control I thus acquired over the thoughtless impulses which make us commit so many follies gained me the admirable presence of mind you all know."

"How deeply I pity the second!" exclaimed the Baronne de Nucingen.

A scarcely perceptible smile on de Marsay's pale lips made Delphine de Nucingen color.

"How we do forget!" said the Baron de Nucingen.

The great banker's simplicity was so extremely droll, that his wife, who was de Marsay's "second," could not help laughing like every one else.

"You are all ready to condemn the woman," said Lady Dudley. "Well, I quite understand that she did not regard her marriage as an act of inconstancy. Men will never distinguish between constancy and fidelity.--I know the woman whose story Monsieur de Marsay has told us, and she is one of the last of your truly great ladies."

"Alas! my lady, you are right," replied de Marsay. "For very nearly fifty years we have been looking on at the progressive ruin of all social distinctions. We ought to have saved our women from this great wreck, but the Civil Code has swept its leveling influence over their heads. However terrible the words, they must be spoken: Duchesses are vanishing, and marquises too! As to the baronesses--I must apologize to Madame de Nucingen, who will become a countess when her husband is made a peer of France--baronesses have never succeeded in getting people to take them seriously."

"Aristocracy begins with the viscountess," said Blondet with a smile.

"Countesses will survive," said de Marsay. "An elegant woman will be more or less of a countess--a countess of the Empire or of yesterday, a countess of the old block, or, as they say in Italy, a countess by courtesy. But as to the great lady, she died out with the dignified splendor of the last century, with powder, patches, high-heeled slippers, and stiff bodices with a delta stomacher of bows. Duchesses in these days can pass through a door without any need to widen it for their hoops. The Empire saw the last of gowns with trains! I am still puzzled to understand how a sovereign who wished to see his drawing-room swept by ducal satin and velvet did not make indestructible laws. Napoleon never guessed the results of the Code he was so proud of. That man, by creating duchesses, founded the race of our 'ladies' of to-day--the indirect offspring of his legislation."

"It was logic, handled as a hammer by boys just out of school and by obscure journalists, which demolished the splendors of the social state," said the Comte de Vandenesse. "In these days every rogue who can hold his head straight in his collar, cover his manly bosom with half an ell of satin by way of a cuirass, display a brow where apocryphal genius gleams under curling locks, and strut in a pair of patent-leather pumps graced by silk socks which cost six francs, screws his eye-glass into one of his eye-sockets by puckering up his cheek, and whether he be an attorney's clerk, a contractor's son, or a banker's bastard, he stares impertinently at the prettiest duchess, appraises her as she walks downstairs, and says to his friend--dressed by Buisson, as we all are, and mounted in patent-leather like any duke himself--'There, my boy, that is a perfect lady.'"

"You have not known how to form a party," said Lord Dudley; "it will be a long time yet before you have a policy. You talk a great deal in France about organizing labor, and you have not yet organized property. So this is what happens: Any duke--and even in the time of Louis XVIII. and Charles X. there were some left who had two hundred thousand francs a year, a magnificent residence, and a sumptuous train of servants--well, such a duke could live like a great lord. The last of these great gentlemen in France was the Prince de Talleyrand.--This duke leaves four children, two of them girls. Granting that he has great luck in marrying them all well, each of these descendants will have but sixty or eighty thousand francs a year now; each is the father or mother of children, and consequently obliged to live with the strictest economy in a flat on the ground floor or first floor of a large house. Who knows if they may not even be hunting a fortune? Henceforth the eldest son's wife, a duchess in name only, has no carriage, no people, no opera-box, no time to herself. She has not her own rooms in the family mansion, nor her fortune, nor her pretty toys; she is buried in trade; she buys socks for her dear little children, nurses them herself, and keeps an eye on her girls, whom she no longer sends to school at a convent. Thus your noblest dames have been turned into worthy brood-hens."

"Alas! it is true," said Joseph Bridau. "In our day we cannot show those beautiful flowers of womanhood which graced the golden ages of the French Monarchy. The great lady's fan is broken. A woman has nothing now to blush for; she need not slander or whisper, hide her face or reveal it. A fan is of no use now but for fanning herself. When once a thing is no more than what it is, it is too useful to be a form of luxury."

"Everything in France has aided and abetted the 'perfect lady,'" said Daniel d'Arthez. "The aristocracy has acknowledged her by retreating to the recesses of its landed estates, where it has hidden itself to die--emigrating inland before the march of ideas, as of old to foreign lands before that of the masses. The women who could have founded European *salons*, could have guided opinion and turned it inside out like a glove, could have ruled the world by ruling the men of art or of intellect who ought to have ruled it, have committed the blunder of abandoning their ground; they were ashamed of having to fight against the citizen class drunk with power, and rushing out on to the stage of the world, there to be cut to pieces perhaps by the barbarians who are at its heels. Hence, where the middle class insist on seeing princesses, these are really only ladylike young women. In these days princes can find no great ladies whom they may compromise; they cannot even confer honor on a woman taken up at random. The Duc de Bourbon was the last prince to avail himself of this privilege."

"And God alone knows how dearly he paid for it," said Lord Dudley.

"Nowadays princes have lady-like wives, obliged to share their opera-box with other ladies; royal favor could not raise them higher by a hair's breadth; they glide unremarkable between the waters of the citizen class and those of the nobility--

not altogether noble nor altogether **bourgeoises**," said the Marquise de Rochegude acridly.

"The press has fallen heir to the Woman," exclaimed Rastignac. "She no longer has the quality of a spoken **feuilleton**--delightful calumnies graced by elegant language. We read **feuilletons** written in a dialect which changes every three years, society papers about as mirthful as an undertaker's mute, and as light as the lead of their type. French conversation is carried on from one end of the country to the other in a revolutionary jargon, through long columns of type printed in old mansions where a press groans in the place where formerly elegant company used to meet."

"The knell of the highest society is tolling," said a Russian Prince. "Do you hear it? And the first stroke is your modern word **lady**."

"You are right, Prince," said de Marsay. "The 'perfect lady,' issuing from the ranks of the nobility, or sprouting from the citizen class, and the product of every soil, even of the provinces is the expression of these times, a last remaining embodiment of good taste, grace, wit, and distinction, all combined, but dwarfed. We shall see no more great ladies in France, but there will be 'ladies' for a long time, elected by public opinion to form an upper chamber of women, and who will be among the fair sex what a 'gentleman' is in England."

"And that they call progress!" exclaimed Mademoiselle des Touches. "I should like to know where the progress lies?"

"Why, in this," said Madame de Nucingen. "Formerly a woman might have the voice of a fish-seller, the walk of a grenadier, the face of an impudent courtesan, her hair too high on her forehead, a large foot, a thick hand--she was a great lady in spite of it all; but in these days, even if she were a Montmorency--if a Montmorency would ever be such a creature--she would not be a lady."

"But what do you mean by a 'perfect lady'?" asked Count Adam Laginski.

"She is a modern product, a deplorable triumph of the elective system as applied to the fair sex," said the Minister. "Every revolution has a word of its own which epitomizes and depicts it."

"You are right," said the Russian, who had come to make a literary reputation in Paris. "The explanation of certain words added from time to time to your beautiful language would make a magnificent history. **Organize**, for instance, is the word of the Empire, and sums up Napoleon completely."

"But all that does not explain what is meant by a lady!" the young Pole exclaimed, with some impatience.

"Well, I will tell you," said Emile Blondet to Count Adam. "One fine morning you go for a saunter in Paris. It is past two, but five has not yet struck. You see a woman coming towards you; your first glance at her is like the preface to a good book, it leads you to expect a world of elegance and refinement. Like a botanist over hill and dale in his pursuit of plants, among the vulgarities of Paris life you have at last found a rare flower. This woman is attended by two very distinguished-looking men, of whom one, at any rate, wears an order; or else a servant out of livery follows her at a distance of ten yards. She displays no gaudy colors, no open-worked stockings, no over-elaborate waist-buckle, no embroidered frills to her drawers fussing round her ankles. You will see that she is shod with prunella shoes, with sandals crossed over extremely fine cotton stockings, or plain gray silk stockings; or perhaps she wears boots of the most exquisite simplicity. You notice that her gown is made of a neat and inexpensive material, but made in a way that surprises more than one woman of the middle class; it is almost always a long pelisse, with bows to fasten it, and neatly bound with fine cord or an imperceptible braid. The Unknown has a way of her own in wrapping herself in her shawl or mantilla; she knows how to draw it round her from her hips to her neck, outlining a carapace, as it were, which would make an ordinary woman look like a turtle, but which in her sets off the most beautiful forms while concealing them. How does she do it? This secret she keeps, though unguarded by any patent.

"As she walks she gives herself a little concentric and harmonious twist, which makes her supple or dangerous slenderness writhe under the stuff, as a snake does under the green gauze of trembling grass. Is it to an angel or a devil that she owes the graceful undulation which plays under her long black silk cape, stirs its lace frill, sheds an airy balm, and what I should like to call the breeze of a Parisienne? You may recognize over her arms, round her waist, about her throat, a science of drapery recalling the antique Mnemosyne.

"Oh! how thoroughly she understands the *cut* of her gait--forgive the expression. Study the way she puts her foot forward moulding her skirt with such a decent preciseness that the passer-by is filled with admiration, mingled with desire, but subdued by deep respect. When an Englishwoman attempts this step, she looks like a grenadier marching forward to attack a redoubt. The women of Paris have a genius for walking. The municipality really owed them asphalt footwalks.

"Our Unknown jostles no one. If she wants to pass, she waits with proud humility till some one makes way. The distinction peculiar to a well-bred woman betrays itself, especially in the way she holds her shawl or cloak crossed over her bosom. Even as she walks she has a little air of serene dignity, like Raphael's Madonnas in their frames. Her aspect, at once quiet and disdainful, makes the most insolent dandy step aside for her.

"Her bonnet, remarkable for its simplicity, is trimmed with crisp ribbons; there may be flowers in it, but the cleverest of such women wear only bows. Feathers demand a carriage; flowers are too showy. Beneath it you see the fresh unworn face of a woman who, without conceit, is sure of herself; who looks at nothing, and sees everything; whose vanity, satiated by being constantly gratified, stamps her face with an indifference which piques your curiosity. She knows that she is looked at, she knows that everybody, even women, turn round to see her again. And she threads her way through Paris like a gossamer, spotless and pure.

"This delightful species affects the hottest latitudes, the cleanest longitudes of Paris; you will meet her between the 10th and 110th Arcade of the Rue de Rivoli; along the line of the Boulevards from the equator of the Passage des Panoramas, where the products of India flourish, where the warmest creations of industry are displayed, to the Cape of the Madeleine; in the least muddy districts of the citizen quarters, between No. 30 and No. 130 of the Rue du Faubourg Saint-Honore. During the winter, she haunts the terrace of the Feuillants, but not the asphalt pavement that lies parallel. According to the weather, she may be seen flying in the Avenue of the Champs-Elysees, which is bounded on the east by the Place Louis XV., on the west by the Avenue de Marigny, to the south by the road, to the north by the gardens of the Faubourg Saint-Honore. Never is this pretty variety of woman to be seen in the hyperborean regions of the Rue Saint-Denis, never in the Kamtschatka of miry, narrow, commercial streets, never anywhere in bad weather. These flowers of Paris, blooming only in Oriental weather, perfume the highways; and after five o'clock fold up like morning-glory flowers. The women you will see later, looking a little like them, are would-be ladies; while the fair Unknown, your Beatrice of a day, is a 'perfect lady.'

"It is not very easy for a foreigner, my dear Count, to recognize the differences by which the observer *emeritus* distinguishes them--women are such consummate actresses; but they are glaring in the eyes of Parisians: hooks ill fastened, strings showing loops of rusty-white tape through a gaping slit in the back, rubbed shoe-leather, ironed bonnet-strings, an over-full skirt, an over-tight waist. You will see a certain effort in the intentional droop of the eyelid. There is something conventional in the attitude.

"As to the *bourgeoise*, the citizen womankind, she cannot possibly be mistaken for the spell cast over you by the Unknown. She is bustling, and goes out in all weathers, trots about, comes, goes, gazes, does not know whether she will or will not go into a shop. Where the lady knows just what she wants and what she is doing, the townswoman is undecided, tucks up her skirts to cross a gutter, dragging a child by the hand, which compels her to look out for the vehicles; she is a mother in public, and talks to her daughter; she carries money in her bag, and has open-work stockings on her feet; in winter, she wears a boa over her fur cloak; in summer, a shawl and a scarf; she is accomplished in the redundancies of dress.

"You will meet the fair Unknown again at the Italiens, at the Opera, at a ball. She will then appear under such a different aspect that you would think them two beings devoid of any analogy. The woman has emerged from those mysterious garments like a butterfly from its silky cocoon. She serves up, like some rare dainty, to your lavished eyes, the forms which her bodice scarcely revealed in the morning. At the theatre she never mounts higher than the second tier, excepting at the Italiens. You can there watch at your leisure the studied deliberateness of her movements. The enchanting deceiver plays off all the little political artifices of her sex so naturally as to exclude all idea of art or premeditation. If she has a royally beautiful hand, the most perspicacious beholder will believe that it is absolutely necessary that she should twist, or refix, or push aside the ringlet or curl she plays with. If she has some dignity of profile, you will be persuaded that she is giving irony or grace to what she says to her neighbor, sitting in such a position as to produce the magical effect of the 'lost profile,' so dear to great painters, by which the cheek catches the high light, the nose is shown in clear outline, the nostrils are transparently rosy, the forehead squarely modeled, the eye has its spangle of fire, but fixed on space, and the white roundness of the chin is accentuated by a line of light. If she has a pretty foot, she will throw herself on a sofa with the coquettish grace of a cat in the sunshine, her feet outstretched without your feeling that her attitude is anything but the most charming model ever given to a sculptor by lassitude.

"Only the perfect lady is quite at her ease in full dress; nothing inconveniences her. You will never see her, like the woman of the citizen class, pulling up a refractory shoulder-strap, or pushing down a rebellious whalebone, or looking whether her tucker is doing its office of faithful guardian to two treasures of dazzling whiteness, or glancing in the mirrors to see if her head-dress is keeping its place. Her toilet is always in harmony with her character; she had had time to study herself, to learn what becomes her, for she has long known what does not suit her. You will not find her as you go out; she vanishes before the end of the play. If by chance she is to be seen, calm and stately, on the stairs, she is experiencing some violent emotion; she has to bestow a glance, to receive a promise. Perhaps she goes down so slowly on purpose to gratify the vanity of a slave whom she sometimes obeys. If your meeting takes place at a ball or an evening party, you will gather the honey, natural or affected of her insinuating voice; her empty words will enchant you, and she will know how to give them the value of thought by her inimitable bearing."

"To be such a woman, is it not necessary to be very clever?" asked the Polish Count.

"It is necessary to have great taste," replied the Princesse de Cadignan.

"And in France taste is more than cleverness," said the Russian.

"This woman's cleverness is the triumph of a purely plastic art," Blondet went on. "You will not know what she said, but you will be fascinated. She will toss her head, or gently shrug her white shoulders; she will gild an insignificant speech with a charming pout and smile; or throw a Voltairean epigram into an 'Indeed!' an 'Ah!' a 'What then!' A jerk of her head will be her most pertinent form of questioning; she will give meaning to the movement by which she twirls a vinaigrette hanging to her finger by a ring. She gets an artificial grandeur out of superlative trivialities; she simply drops her hand impressively, letting it fall over the arm of her chair as dewdrops hang on the cup of a flower, and all is said--she has pronounced judgment beyond appeal, to the apprehension of the most obtuse. She knows how to listen to you; she gives you the opportunity of shining, and--I ask your modesty--those moments are rare?"

The candid simplicity of the young Pole, to whom Blondet spoke, made all the party shout with laughter.

"Now, you will not talk for half-an-hour with a **bourgeoise** without her alluding to her husband in one way or another," Blondet went on with unperturbed gravity; "whereas, even if you know that your lady is married, she will have the delicacy to conceal her husband so effectually that it will need the enterprise of Christopher Columbus to discover him. Often you will fail in the attempt single-handed. If you have had no opportunity of inquiring, towards the end of the evening you detect her gazing fixedly at a middle-aged man wearing a decoration, who bows and goes out. She has ordered her carriage, and goes.

"You are not the rose, but you have been with the rose, and you go to bed under the golden canopy of a delicious dream, which will last perhaps after Sleep, with his heavy finger, has opened the ivory gates of the temple of dreams.

"The lady, when she is at home, sees no one before four; she is shrewd enough always to keep you waiting. In her house you will find everything in good taste; her luxury is for hourly use, and duly renewed; you will see nothing under glass shades, no rags of wrappings hanging about, and looking like a pantry. You will find the staircase warmed. Flowers on all sides will charm your sight--flowers, the only gift she accepts, and those only from certain people, for nosegays live but a day; they give pleasure, and must be replaced; to her they are, as in the East, a symbol and a promise. The costly toys of fashion lie about, but not so as to suggest a museum or a curiosity shop. You will find her sitting by the fire in a low chair, from which she will not rise to greet you. Her talk will not now be what it was at the ball; there she was our creditor; in her own home she owes you the pleasure of her wit. These are the shades of which the lady is a marvelous mistress. What she likes in you is a man to swell her circle, an object for the cares and attentions which such women are now happy to bestow. Therefore, to attract you to her drawing-room, she will be bewitchingly charming. This especially is where you feel how isolated women are nowadays, and why they want a little world of their own, to which they may seem a constellation. Conversation is impossible without generalities."

"Yes," said de Marsay, "you have truly hit the fault of our age. The epigram--a volume in a word--no longer strikes, as it did in the eighteenth century, at persons or at things, but at squalid events, and it dies in a day."

"Hence," said Blondet, "the intelligence of the lady, if she has any, consists in casting doubts on everything. Here lies the great difference between two women; the townswoman is certainly virtuous; the lady does not know yet whether she is, or whether she always will be; she hesitates and struggles where the other refuses point-blank and falls full length. This hesitancy in everything is one of the last graces left to her by our horrible times. She rarely goes to church, but she will talk to you of religion; and if you have the good taste to affect Free-thought, she will try to convert you, for you will have opened the way for the stereotyped phrases, the head-shaking and gestures understood by all these women: 'For shame! I thought you had too much sense to attack religion. Society is tottering, and you deprive it of its support. Why, religion at this moment means you and me; it is property, and the future of our children! Ah! let us not be selfish! Individualism is the disease of the age, and religion is the only remedy; it unites families which your laws put asunder,' and so forth. Then she plunges into some neo-Christian speech sprinkled with political notions which is neither Catholic nor Protestant--but moral? Oh! deuced moral!--in which you may recognize a fag end of every material woven by modern doctrines, at loggerheads together."

The women could not help laughing at the airs by which Blondet illustrated his satire.

"This explanation, dear Count Adam," said Blondet, turning to the Pole, "will have proved to you that the 'perfect lady' represents the intellectual no less than the political muddle, just as she is surrounded by the showy and not very lasting products of an industry which is always aiming at destroying its work in order to replace it by something else. When you leave her you say to yourself: She certainly has superior ideas! And you believe it all the more because she will have sounded your heart with a delicate touch, and have asked you your secrets; she affects ignorance, to learn everything; there are some things she never knows, not even when she knows them. You alone will be uneasy, you will know nothing of the state of her heart. The great ladies of old flaunted their love-affairs, with newspapers and advertisements; in these days the lady has her little passion neatly ruled like a sheet of music with its crotchets and quavers and minims, its rests, its pauses, its sharps to sign the key. A mere weak women, she is anxious not to compromise her love, or her husband, or the future of her children. Name, position, and fortune are no longer flags so respected as to protect all kinds of merchandise on board. The whole aristocracy no longer advances in a body to screen the lady. She has not, like the great lady of the past, the demeanor of lofty antagonism; she can crush nothing under foot, it is she who would be crushed. Thus she is apt at Jesuitical *mezzo termine*, she is a creature of equivocal compromises, of guarded proprieties, of anonymous passions steered between two reef-bound shores. She is as much afraid of her servants as an Englishwoman who lives in dread of a trial in the divorce-court. This woman--so free at a ball, so attractive out walking--is a slave at home; she is never independent but in perfect privacy, or theoretically. She must preserve herself in her position as a lady. This is her task.

"For in our day a woman repudiated by her husband, reduced to a meagre allowance, with no carriage, no luxury, no opera-box, none of the divine accessories of the toilet, is no longer a wife, a maid, or a townswoman; she is adrift, and becomes a chattel. The Carmelites will not receive a married woman; it would be bigamy. Would her lover still have anything to say to her? That is the question. Thus your perfect lady may perhaps give occasion to calumny, never to slander."

"It is all so horribly true," said the Princesse de Cadignan.

"And so," said Blondet, "our 'perfect lady' lives between English hypocrisy and the delightful frankness of the eighteenth century--a bastard system, symptomatic of an age in which nothing that grows up is at all like the thing that has vanished, in which transition leads nowhere, everything is a matter of degree; all the great figures shrink into the background, and distinction is purely personal. I am fully convinced that it is impossible for a woman, even if she were born close to a throne, to acquire before the age of five-and-twenty the encyclopaedic knowledge of trifles, the practice of manoeuvring, the important small things, the musical tones and harmony of coloring, the angelic bedevilments and innocent cunning, the speech and the silence, the seriousness and the banter, the wit and the obtuseness, the diplomacy and the ignorance which make up the perfect lady."

"And where, in accordance with the sketch you have drawn," said Mademoiselle des Touches to Emile Blondet, "would you class the female author? Is she a perfect lady, a woman *comme il faut*?"

"When she has no genius, she is a woman *comme il n'en faut pas*," Blondet replied, emphasizing the words with a stolen glance, which might make them seem praise frankly addressed to Camille Maupin. "This epigram is not mine, but Napoleon's," he added.

"You need not owe Napoleon any grudge on that score," said Canalis, with an emphatic tone and gesture. "It was one of his weaknesses to be jealous of literary genius--for he had his mean points. Who will ever explain, depict, or understand Napoleon? A man represented with his arms folded, and who did everything, who was the greatest force ever known, the most concentrated, the most mordant, the most acid of all forces; a singular genius who carried armed civilization in every direction without fixing it anywhere; a man who could do everything because he willed everything; a prodigious phenomenon of will, conquering an illness by a battle, and yet doomed to die of disease in bed after living in the midst of ball and bullets; a man with a code and a sword in his brain, word and deed; a clear-sighted spirit that foresaw everything but his own fall; a capricious politician who risked men by handfuls out of economy, and who spared three heads --those of Talleyrand, of Pozzo de Borgo, and of Metternich, diplomatists whose death would have saved the French Empire, and who seemed to him of greater weight than thousands of soldiers; a man to whom nature, as a rare privilege, had given a heart in a frame of bronze; mirthful and kind at midnight amid women, and next morning manipulating Europe as a young girl might amuse herself by splashing water in her bath! Hypocritical and generous; loving tawdriness and simplicity; devoid of taste, but protecting the arts; and in spite of these antitheses, really great in everything by instinct or by temperament; Caesar at five-and-twenty, Cromwell at thirty; and then, like my grocer buried in Pere Lachaise, a good husband and a good father. In short, he improvised public works, empires, kings, codes, verses, a romance--and all with more range than precision. Did he not aim at making all Europe France? And after making us weigh on the earth in such a way as to change the laws of gravitation, he left us poorer than on the day when he first laid hands on us; while he, who had taken an empire by his name, lost his name on the frontier of his empire in a sea of blood and soldiers. A man all thought and all action, who comprehended Desaix and Fouche."

"All despotism and all justice at the right moments. The true king!" said de Marsay.

"Ah! vat a pleashre it is to dichest vile you talk," said Baron de Nucingen.

"But do you suppose that the treat we are giving you is a common one?" asked Joseph Bridau. "If you had to pay for the charms of conversation as you do for those of dancing or of music, your fortune would be inadequate! There is no second performance of the same flash of wit."

"And are we really so much deteriorated as these gentlemen think?" said the Princesse de Cadignan, addressing the women with a smile at once sceptical and ironical. "Because, in these days, under a regime which makes everything small, you prefer small dishes, small rooms, small pictures, small articles, small newspapers, small books, does that prove that women too have grown smaller? Why should the human heart change because you change your coat? In all ages the passions remain the same. I know cases of beautiful devotion, of sublime sufferings, which lack the publicity--the glory, if you choose--which formerly gave lustre to the errors of some women. But though one may not have saved a King of France, one is not the less an Agnes Sorel. Do you believe that our dear Marquise d'Espard is not the peer of Madame Doublet, or Madame du Deffant, in whose rooms so much evil was spoken and done? Is not Taglioni a match for Camargo? or Malibran the equal of Saint-Huberti? Are not our poets superior to those of the eighteenth century? If at this moment, through the fault of the Grocers who govern us, we have not a style of our own, had not the Empire its distinguishing stamp as the age of Louis XV. had, and was not its splendor fabulous? Have the sciences lost anything?"

"I am quite of your opinion, madame; the women of this age are truly great," replied the Comte de Vandenesse. "When posterity shall have followed us, will not Madame Recamier appear in proportions as fine as those of the most beautiful women of the past? We have made so much history that historians will be lacking. The age of Louis XIV. had but one Madame de Sevigne; we have a thousand now in Paris who certainly write better than she did, and who do not publish their letters. Whether the Frenchwoman be called 'perfect lady,' or great lady, she will always be *the* woman among women.

"Emile Blondet has given us a picture of the fascinations of a woman of the day; but, at need, this creature who bridles or shows off, who chirps out the ideas of Mr. This and Mr. That, would be heroic. And it must be said, your faults, mesdames, are all the more poetical, because they must always and under all circumstances be surrounded by greater perils. I have seen much of the world, I have studied it perhaps too late; but in cases where the illegality of your feelings might be excused, I have always observed the effects of I know not what chance--which you may call Providence--inevitably overwhelming such as we consider light women."

"I hope," said Madame de Vandenesse, "that we can be great in other ways----"

"Oh, let the Comte de Vandenesse preach to us!" exclaimed Madame de Serizy.

"With all the more reason because he has preached a great deal by example," said the Baronne de Nucingen.

"On my honor!" said General de Montriveau, "in all the dramas--a word you are very fond of," he said, looking at Blondet--"in which the finger of God has been visible, the most frightful I ever knew was very near being by my act----"

"Well, tell us all about it!" cried Lady Barimore; "I love to shudder!"

"It is the taste of a virtuous woman," replied de Marsay, looking at Lord Dudley's lovely daughter.

"During the campaign of 1812," General de Montriveau began, "I was the involuntary cause of a terrible disaster which may be of use to you, Doctor Bianchon," turning to me, "since, while devoting yourself to the human body, you concern yourself a good deal with the mind; it may tend to solve some of the problems of the will.

"I was going through my second campaign; I enjoyed danger, and laughed at everything, like the young and foolish lieutenant of artillery that I was. When we reached the Beresina, the army had, as you know, lost all discipline, and had forgotten military obedience. It was a medley of men of all nations, instinctively making their way from north to south. The soldiers would drive a general in rags and bare-foot away from their fire if he brought neither wood nor victuals. After the passage of this famous river disorder did not diminish. I had come quietly and alone, without food, out of the marshes of Zembin, and was wandering in search of a house where I might be taken in. Finding none or driven away from those I came across, happily towards evening I perceived a wretched little Polish farm, of which nothing can give you any idea unless you have seen the wooden houses of Lower Normandy, or the poorest farm-buildings of la Beauce. These dwellings consist of a single room, with one end divided off by a wooden partition, the smaller division serving as a store-room for forage.

"In the darkness of twilight I could just see a faint smoke rising above this house. Hoping to find there some comrades more compassionate than those I had hitherto addressed, I boldly walked as far as the farm. On going in, I found the table laid. Several officers, and with them a woman--a common sight enough--were eating potatoes, some horseflesh broiled over the charcoal, and some frozen beetroots. I recognized among the company two or three artillery captains of the regiment in which I had first served. I was welcomed with a shout of acclamation, which would have amazed me greatly on the other side of the Beresina; but at this moment the cold was less intense; my fellow-officers were resting, they were warm, they had food, and the room, strewn with trusses of straw, gave the promise of a delightful night. We did not ask for so much in those days. My comrades could be philanthropists *gratis*--one of the commonest ways of being philanthropic. I sat down to eat on one of the bundles of straw.

"At the end of the table, by the side of the door opening into the smaller room full of straw and hay, sat my old colonel, one of the most extraordinary men I ever saw among all the mixed collection of men it has been my lot to meet. He was an Italian. Now, whenever human nature is truly fine in the lands of the South, it is really sublime. I do not know whether you have ever observed the extreme fairness of Italians when they are fair. It is exquisite, especially under an artificial light. When I read the fantastical portrait of Colonel Oudet sketched by Charles Nodier, I found my own sensations in every one of his elegant phrases. Italian, then, as were most of the officers of his regiment, which had, in fact, been borrowed by the Emperor from Eugene's army, my colonel was a tall man, at least eight or nine inches above the standard, and was admirably proportioned--a little stout perhaps, but prodigiously powerful, active, and clean-limbed as a greyhound. His black hair in abundant curls showed up his complexion, as white as a woman's; he had small hands, a shapely foot, a pleasant mouth, and an aquiline nose delicately formed, of which the tip used to become naturally pinched and white whenever he was angry, as happened often. His irascibility was so far beyond belief that I will tell you nothing about it; you will have the opportunity of judging of it. No one could be calm in his presence. I alone, perhaps, was not afraid of him; he had indeed taken such a singular fancy to me that he thought everything I did right. When he was in a rage his brow was knit and the muscles of the middle of his forehead set in a delta, or, to be more explicit, in Redgauntlet's horseshoe. This mark was, perhaps, even more terrifying than the magnetic flashes of his blue eyes. His whole frame quivered, and his strength, great as it was in his normal state, became almost unbounded.

"He spoke with a strong guttural roll. His voice, at least as powerful as that of Charles Nordier's Oudet, threw an incredible fulness of tone into the syllable or the consonant in which this burr was sounded. Though this faulty pronunciation was at times a grace, when commanding his men, or when he was excited, you cannot imagine, unless you had heard it, what force was expressed by this accent, which at Paris is so common. When the Colonel was quiescent, his blue eyes were angelically sweet, and his smooth brow had a most charming expression. On parade, or with the army of Italy, not a man could compare with him. Indeed, d'Orsay himself, the handsome d'Orsay, was eclipsed by our colonel on the occasion of the last review held by Napoleon before the invasion of Russia.

"Everything was in contrasts in this exceptional man. Passion lives on contrast. Hence you need not ask whether he exerted over women the irresistible influences to which our nature yields"--and the general looked at the Princesse de Cadignan--"as vitreous matter is moulded under the pipe of the glass-blower; still, by a singular fatality--an observer might perhaps explain the phenomenon--the Colonel was not a lady-killer, or was indifferent to such successes.

"To give you an idea of his violence, I will tell you in a few words what I once saw him do in a paroxysm of fury. We were dragging our guns up a very narrow road, bordered by a somewhat high slope on one side, and by thickets on the other. When we were half-way up we met another regiment of artillery, its colonel marching at the head. This colonel wanted to make the captain who was at the head of our foremost battery back down again. The captain, of course, refused; but the colonel of the other regiment signed to his foremost battery to advance, and in spite of the care the driver took to keep among the scrub, the wheel of the first gun struck our captain's right leg and broke it, throwing him over on the near side of his horse. All this was the work of a moment. Our Colonel, who was but a little way off, guessed that there was a quarrel; he galloped up, riding among the guns at the risk of falling with his horse's four feet in the air, and reached the spot, face to face with the other colonel, at the very moment when the captain fell, calling out 'Help!' No, our Italian colonel was no longer human! Foam like the froth of champagne rose to his lips; he roared inarticulately like a lion. Incapable of uttering a word, or even a cry, he made a terrific signal to his antagonist, pointing to the wood and drawing his sword. The two colonels went aside. In two seconds we saw our Colonel's opponent stretched on the ground, his skull split in two. The soldiers of his regiment backed --yes, by heaven, and pretty quickly too.

"The captain, who had been so nearly crushed, and who lay yelping in the puddle where the gun carriage had thrown him, had an Italian wife, a beautiful Sicilian of Messina, who was not indifferent to our Colonel. This circumstance had aggravated his rage. He was pledged to protect the husband, bound to defend him as he would have defended the woman herself.

"Now, in the hovel beyond Zembin, where I was so well received, this captain was sitting opposite to me, and his wife was at the other end of the table, facing the Colonel. This Sicilian was a little woman named Rosina, very dark, but with all the fire of the Southern sun in her black almond-shaped eyes. At this moment she was deplorably thin; her face was covered with dust, like fruit exposed to the drought of a highroad. Scarcely clothed in rags, exhausted by marches, her hair in disorder, and clinging together under a piece of a shawl tied close over her head, still she had the graces of a woman; her movements were engaging, her small rose mouth and white teeth, the outline of her features and figure, charms which misery, cold, and neglect had not altogether defaced, still suggested love to any man who could think of a woman. Rosina had one of those frames which are fragile in appearance, but wiry and full of spring. Her husband, a gentleman of Piedmont, had a face expressive of ironical simplicity, if it is allowable to ally the two words. Brave and well informed, he seemed to know nothing of the connections which had subsisted between his wife and the Colonel for three years past. I ascribed this unconcern to Italian manners, or to some domestic secret; yet there was in the man's countenance one feature which always filled me with involuntary distrust. His under lip, which was thin and very restless, turned down at the corners instead of turning up, and this, as I thought, betrayed a streak of cruelty in a character which seemed so phlegmatic and indolent.

"As you may suppose the conversation was not very sparkling when I went in.

My weary comrades ate in silence; of course, they asked me some questions, and we related our misadventures, mingled with reflections on the campaign, the generals, their mistakes, the Russians, and the cold. A minute after my arrival the colonel, having finished his meagre meal, wiped his moustache, bid us good-night, shot a black look at the Italian woman, saying, 'Rosina?' and then, without waiting for a reply, went into the little barn full of hay, to bed. The meaning of the Colonel's utterance was self-evident. The young wife replied by an indescribable gesture, expressing all the annoyance she could not feel at seeing her thralldom thus flaunted without human decency, and the offence to her dignity as a woman, and to her husband. But there was, too, in the rigid setting of her features and the tight knitting of her brows a sort of presentiment; perhaps she foresaw her fate. Rosina remained quietly in her place.

"A minute later, and apparently when the Colonel was snug in his couch of straw or hay, he repeated, 'Rosina?'

"The tone of this second call was even more brutally questioning than the first. The Colonel's strong burr, and the length which the Italian language allows to be given to vowels and the final syllable, concentrated all the man's despotism, impatience, and strength of will. Rosina turned pale, but she rose, passed behind us, and went to the Colonel.

"All the party sat in utter silence; I, unluckily, after looking at them all, began to laugh, and then they all laughed too.--'*Tu ridi?* --you laugh?' said the husband.

"'On my honor, old comrade,' said I, becoming serious again, 'I confess that I was wrong; I ask your pardon a thousand times, and if you are not satisfied by my apologies I am ready to give you satisfaction.'

"'Oh! it is not you who are wrong, it is I!' he replied coldly.

"Thereupon we all lay down in the room, and before long all were sound asleep.

"Next morning each one, without rousing his neighbor or seeking companionship, set out again on his way, with that selfishness which made our rout one of the most horrible dramas of self-seeking, melancholy, and horror which ever was enacted under heaven. Nevertheless, at about seven or eight hundred paces from our shelter we, most of us, met again and walked on together, like geese led in flocks by a child's wilful tyranny. The same necessity urged us all.

"Having reached a knoll where we could still see the farmhouse where we had spent the night, we heard sounds resembling the roar of lions in the desert, the bellowing of bulls--no, it was a noise which can be compared to no known cry. And yet, mingling with this horrible and ominous roar, we could hear a woman's feeble scream. We all looked round, seized by I know not what impulse of terror; we no longer saw the house, but a huge bonfire. The farmhouse had been barricaded, and was in flames. Swirls of smoke borne on the wind brought us hoarse cries and an indescribable pungent smell. A few yards behind, the captain was quietly approaching to join our caravan; we gazed at him in silence, for no one dared question him; but he, understanding our curiosity, pointed to his breast with the forefinger of his right hand, and, waving the left in the direction of the fire, he said, '**Son'io**.'

"We all walked on without saying a word to him."

"There is nothing more terrible than the revolt of a sheep," said de Marsay.

"It would be frightful to let us leave with this horrible picture in our memory," said Madame de Montcornet. "I shall dream of it----"

"And what was the punishment of Monsieur de Marsay's 'First'?" said Lord Dudley, smiling.

"When the English are in jest, their foils have the buttons on," said Blondet.

"Monsieur Bianchon can tell us, for he saw her dying," replied de Marsay, turning to me.

"Yes," said I; "and her end was one of the most beautiful I ever saw. The Duke and I had spent the night by the dying woman's pillow; pulmonary consumption, in the last stage, left no hope; she had taken the sacrament the day before. The Duke had fallen asleep. The Duchess, waking at about four in the morning, signed to me in the most touching way, with a friendly smile, to bid me leave him to rest, and she meanwhile was about to die. She had become incredibly thin, but her face had preserved its really sublime outline and features. Her pallor made her skin look like porcelain with a light within. Her bright eyes and color contrasted with this languidly elegant complexion, and her countenance was full of expressive calm. She seemed to pity the Duke, and the feeling had its origin in a lofty tenderness which, as death approached, seemed to know no bounds. The silence was absolute. The room, softly lighted by a lamp, looked like every sickroom at the hour of death.

"At this moment the clock struck. The Duke awoke, and was in despair at having fallen asleep. I did not see the gesture of impatience by which he manifested the regret he felt at having lost sight of his wife for a few of the last minutes vouchsafed to him; but it is quite certain that any one but the dying woman might have misunderstood it. A busy statesman, always thinking of the interests of France, the Duke had a thousand odd ways on the surface, such as often lead to a man of genius being mistaken for a madman, and of which the explanation lies in the exquisiteness and exacting needs of their intellect. He came to seat himself in an armchair by his wife's side, and looked fixedly at her. The dying woman put her hand out a little way, took her husband's and clasped it feebly; and in a low but agitated voice she said, 'My poor dear, who is left to understand you now?' Then she died, looking at him."

"The stories the doctor tells us," said the Comte de Vandenesse, "always leave a deep impression."

"But a sweet one," said Mademoiselle des Touches, rising.

PARIS, June 1839-42.

ADDENDUM
The following personages appear in other stories of the Human Comedy.
Bianchon, Horace
Father Goriot
The Atheist's Mass
Cesar Birotteau
The Commission in Lunacy
Lost Illusions
A Distinguished Provincial at Paris
A Bachelor's Establishment
The Secrets of a Princess
The Government Clerks
Pierrette
A Study of Woman
Scenes from a Courtesan's Life
Honorine

The Seamy Side of History
The Magic Skin
A Second Home
A Prince of Bohemia
Letters of Two Brides
The Muse of the Department
The Imaginary Mistress
The Middle Classes
Cousin Betty
The Country Parson In addition, M. Bianchon narrated the following:
La Grande Breteche
Blondet, Emile
Jealousies of a Country Town
A Distinguished Provincial at Paris
Scenes from a Courtesan's Life
Modeste Mignon
The Secrets of a Princess
A Daughter of Eve
The Firm of Nucingen
The Peasantry
Blondet, Virginie (Madame Montcornet)
Jealousies of a Country Town
The Secrets of a Princess
The Peasantry
A Distinguished Provincial at Paris
The Member for Arcis
A Daughter of Eve
Bridau, Joseph
The Purse
A Bachelor's Establishment
A Distinguished Provincial at Paris
A Start in Life
Modeste Mignon

Pierre Grassou
Letters of Two Brides
Cousin Betty
The Member for Arcis
Canalis, Constant-Cyr-Melchior, Baron de
Letters of Two Brides
A Distinguished Provincial at Paris
Modeste Mignon
The Magic Skin
A Start in Life
Beatrix
The Unconscious Humorists
The Member for Arcis
Dudley, Lord
The Lily of the Valley
The Thirteen
A Man of Business
A Daughter of Eve
Espard, Jeanne-Clementine-Athenais de Blamont-Chauvry, Marquise d'
The Commission in Lunacy
A Distinguished Provincial at Paris
Scenes from a Courtesan's Life
Letters of Two Brides
The Gondreville Mystery
The Secrets of a Princess
A Daughter of Eve
Beatrix
Laginski, Comte Adam Mitgislas
The Imaginary Mistress
Cousin Betty
Marsay, Henri de
The Thirteen
The Unconscious Humorists

The Lily of the Valley
Father Goriot
Jealousies of a Country Town
Ursule Mirouet
A Marriage Settlement
Lost Illusions
A Distinguished Provincial at Paris
Letters of Two Brides
The Ball at Sceaux
Modeste Mignon
The Secrets of a Princess
The Gondreville Mystery
A Daughter of Eve
Maufrigneuse, Duchesse de
The Secrets of a Princess
Modeste Mignon
Jealousies of a Country Town
The Muse of the Department
Scenes from a Courtesan's Life
Letters of Two Brides
The Gondreville Mystery
The Member for Arcis
Montriveau, General Marquis Armand de
The Thirteen
Father Goriot
Lost Illusions
A Distinguished Provincial at Paris
Pierrette
The Member for Arcis
Nucingen, Baron Frederic de
The Firm of Nucingen
Father Goriot
Pierrette

Cesar Birotteau
Lost Illusions
A Distinguished Provincial at Paris
Scenes from a Courtesan's Life
The Secrets of a Princess
A Man of Business
Cousin Betty
The Muse of the Department
The Unconscious Humorists
Nucingen, Baronne Delphine de
Father Goriot
The Thirteen
Eugenie Grandet
Cesar Birotteau
Melmoth Reconciled
Lost Illusions
A Distinguished Provincial at Paris
The Commission in Lunacy
Scenes from a Courtesan's Life
Modeste Mignon
The Firm of Nucingen
A Daughter of Eve
The Member for Arcis
Portenduere, Vicomtesse Savinien de
Ursule Mirouet
Beatrix
Rastignac, Eugene de
Father Goriot
A Distinguished Provincial at Paris
Scenes from a Courtesan's Life
The Ball at Sceaux
The Commission in Lunacy
A Study of Woman

The Magic Skin
The Secrets of a Princess
A Daughter of Eve
The Gondreville Mystery
The Firm of Nucingen
Cousin Betty
The Member for Arcis
The Unconscious Humorists
Ronquerolles, Marquis de
The Imaginary Mistress
The Peasantry
Ursule Mirouet
A Woman of Thirty
The Thirteen
The Member for Arcis
Serizy, Comtesse de
A Start in Life
The Thirteen
Ursule Mirouet
A Woman of Thirty
Scenes from a Courtesan's Life
  The Imaginary Mistress
Touches, Mademoiselle Felicite des
Beatrix
Lost Illusions
A Distinguished Provincial at Paris
A Bachelor's Establishment
A Daughter of Eve
Honorine
Beatrix
The Muse of the Department
Vandenesse, Comte Felix de
The Lily of the Valley

Lost Illusions
A Distinguished Provincial at Paris
Cesar Birotteau
Letters of Two Brides
A Start in Life
The Marriage Settlement
The Secrets of a Princess
The Gondreville Mystery
A Daughter of Eve

The Codes Of Hammurabi And Moses
W. W. Davies
QTY

The discovery of the Hammurabi Code is one of the greatest achievements of archaeology, and is of paramount interest, not only to the student of the Bible, but also to all those interested in ancient history...

Religion   **ISBN:** *1-59462-338-4*   **Pages:132**
MSRP $12.95

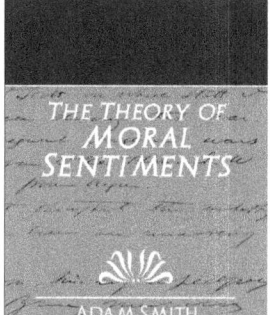

The Theory of Moral Sentiments
Adam Smith
QTY

This work from 1749. contains original theories of conscience amd moral judgment and it is the foundation for systemof morals.

Philosophy   ISBN: *1-59462-777-0*   **Pages:536**
MSRP $19.95

Jessica's First Prayer
Hesba Stretton
QTY

In a screened and secluded corner of one of the many railway-bridges which span the streets of London there could be seen a few years ago, from five o'clock every morning until half past eight, a tidily set-out coffee-stall, consisting of a trestle and board, upon which stood two large tin cans, with a small fire of charcoal burning under each so as to keep the coffee boiling during the early hours of the morning when the work-people were thronging into the city on their way to their daily toil...

Pages:84

Childrens   ISBN: *1-59462-373-2*   *MSRP $9.95*

My Life and Work
Henry Ford
QTY

Henry Ford revolutionized the world with his implementation of mass production for the Model T automobile. Gain valuable business insight into his life and work with his own auto-biography... "We have only started on our development of our country we have not as yet, with all our talk of wonderful progress, done more than scratch the surface. The progress has been wonderful enough but..."

Pages:300

Biographies/   ISBN: *1-59462-198-5*   *MSRP $21.95*

The Art of Cross-Examination
Francis Wellman

QTY

I presume it is the experience of every author, after his first book is published upon an important subject, to be almost overwhelmed with a wealth of ideas and illustrations which could readily have been included in his book, and which to his own mind, at least, seem to make a second edition inevitable. Such certainly was the case with me; and when the first edition had reached its sixth impression in five months, I rejoiced to learn that it seemed to my publishers that the book had met with a sufficiently favorable reception to justify a second and considerably enlarged edition. ...

Reference   ISBN: *1-59462-647-2*

Pages:412

MSRP $19.95

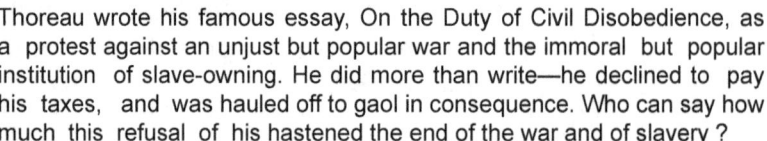

On the Duty of Civil Disobedience
Henry David Thoreau

QTY

Thoreau wrote his famous essay, On the Duty of Civil Disobedience, as a protest against an unjust but popular war and the immoral but popular institution of slave-owning. He did more than write—he declined to pay his taxes, and was hauled off to gaol in consequence. Who can say how much this refusal of his hastened the end of the war and of slavery ?

Law   ISBN: *1-59462-747-9*

Pages:48

MSRP $7.45

Dream Psychology Psychoanalysis for Beginners
Sigmund Freud

QTY

Sigmund Freud, born Sigismund Schlomo Freud (May 6, 1856 - September 23, 1939), was a Jewish-Austrian neurologist and psychiatrist who co-founded the psychoanalytic school of psychology. Freud is best known for his theories of the unconscious mind, especially involving the mechanism of repression; his redefinition of sexual desire as mobile and directed towards a wide variety of objects; and his therapeutic techniques, especially his understanding of transference in the therapeutic relationship and the presumed value of dreams as sources of insight into unconscious desires.

Dream Psychology
Psychoanalysis for Beginners

Sigmund Freud

Psychology   ISBN: *1-59462-905-6*

Pages:196

MSRP $15.45

The Miracle of Right Thought
Orison Swett Marden

QTY

Believe with all of your heart that you will do what you were made to do. When the mind has once formed the habit of holding cheerful, happy, prosperous pictures, it will not be easy to form the opposite habit. It does not matter how improbable or how far away this realization may see, or how dark the prospects may be, if we visualize them as best we can, as vividly as possible, hold tenaciously to them and vigorously struggle to attain them, they will gradually become actualized, realized in the life. But a desire, a longing without endeavor, a yearning abandoned or held indifferently will vanish without realization.

Self Help   ISBN: *1-59462-644-8*

Pages:360

MSRP $25.45

The Rosicrucian Cosmo-Conception Mystic Christianity *by Max Heindel* ISBN: *1-59462-188-8* **$38.95**
The Rosicrucian Cosmo-conception is not dogmatic, neither does it appeal to any other authority than the reason of the student. It is: not controversial, but is: sent forth in the, hope that it may help to clear... New Age/Religion Pages 646

Abandonment To Divine Providence *by Jean-Pierre de Caussade* ISBN: *1-59462-228-0* **$25.95**
"The Rev. Jean Pierre de Caussade was one of the most remarkable spiritual writers of the Society of Jesus in France in the 18th Century. His death took place at Toulouse in 1751. His works have gone through many editions and have been republished... Inspirational/Religion Pages 400

Mental Chemistry *by Charles Haanel* ISBN: *1-59462-192-6* **$23.95**
Mental Chemistry allows the change of material conditions by combining and appropriately utilizing the power of the mind. Much like applied chemistry creates something new and unique out of careful combinations of chemicals the mastery of mental chemistry... New Age Pages 354

The Letters of Robert Browning and Elizabeth Barret Barrett 1845-1846 vol II ISBN: *1-59462-193-4* **$35.95**
by Robert Browning and Elizabeth Barrett Biographies Pages 596

Gleanings In Genesis (volume I) *by Arthur W. Pink* ISBN: *1-59462-130-6* **$27.45**
Appropriately has Genesis been termed "the seed plot of the Bible" for in it we have, in germ form, almost all of the great doctrines which are afterwards fully developed in the books of Scripture which follow... Religion/Inspirational Pages 420

The Master Key *by L. W. de Laurence* ISBN: *1-59462-001-6* **$30.95**
In no branch of human knowledge has there been a more lively increase of the spirit of research during the past few years than in the study of Psychology, Concentration and Mental Discipline. The requests for authentic lessons in Thought Control, Mental Discipline and... New Age/Business Pages 422

The Lesser Key Of Solomon Goetia *by L. W. de Laurence* ISBN: *1-59462-092-X* **$9.95**
This translation of the first book of the "Lernegton" which is now for the first time made accessible to students of Talismanic Magic was done, after careful collation and edition, from numerous Ancient Manuscripts in Hebrew, Latin, and French... New Age/Occult Pages 92

Rubaiyat Of Omar Khayyam *by Edward Fitzgerald* ISBN: *1-59462-332-5* **$13.95**
Edward Fitzgerald, whom the world has already learned, in spite of his own efforts to remain within the shadow of anonymity, to look upon as one of the rarest poets of the century, was born at Bredfield, in Suffolk, on the 31st of March, 1809. He was the third son of John Purcell... Music Pages 172

Ancient Law *by Henry Maine* ISBN: *1-59462-128-4* **$29.95**
The chief object of the following pages is to indicate some of the earliest ideas of mankind, as they are reflected in Ancient Law, and to point out the relation of those ideas to modern thought. Religion/History Pages 452

Far-Away Stories *by William J. Locke* ISBN: *1-59462-129-2* **$19.45**
"Good wine needs no bush, but a collection of mixed vintages does. And this book is just such a collection. Some of the stories I do not want to remain buried for ever in the museum files of dead magazine-numbers an author's not unpardonable vanity..." Fiction Pages 272

Life of David Crockett *by David Crockett* ISBN: *1-59462-250-7* **$27.45**
"Colonel David Crockett was one of the most remarkable men of the times in which he lived. Born in humble life, but gifted with a strong will, an indomitable courage, and unremitting perseverance... Biographies/New Age Pages 424

Lip-Reading *by Edward Nitchie* ISBN: *1-59462-206-X* **$25.95**
Edward B. Nitchie, founder of the New York School for the Hard of Hearing, now the Nitchie School of Lip-Reading, Inc, wrote "LIP-READING Principles and Practice". The development and perfecting of this meritorious work on lip-reading was an undertaking... How-to Pages 400

A Handbook of Suggestive Therapeutics, Applied Hypnotism, Psychic Science ISBN: *1-59462-214-0* **$24.95**
by Henry Munro Health/New Age/Health/Self-help Pages 376

A Doll's House: and Two Other Plays *by Henrik Ibsen* ISBN: *1-59462-112-8* **$19.95**
Henrik Ibsen created this classic when in revolutionary 1848 Rome. Introducing some striking concepts in playwriting for the realist genre, this play has been studied the world over. Fiction/Classics/Plays 308

The Light of Asia *by sir Edwin Arnold* ISBN: *1-59462-204-3* **$13.95**
In this poetic masterpiece, Edwin Arnold describes the life and teachings of Buddha. The man who was to become known as Buddha to the world was born as Prince Gautama of India but he rejected the worldly riches and abandoned the reigns of power when... Religion/History/Biographies Pages 170

The Complete Works of Guy de Maupassant *by Guy de Maupassant* ISBN: *1-59462-157-8* **$16.95**
"For days and days, nights and nights, I had dreamed of that first kiss which was to consecrate our engagement, and I knew not on what spot I should put my lips..." Fiction/Classics Pages 240

The Art of Cross-Examination *by Francis L. Wellman* ISBN: *1-59462-309-0* **$26.95**
Written by a renowned trial lawyer, Wellman imparts his experience and uses case studies to explain how to use psychology to extract desired information through questioning. How-to/Science/Reference Pages 408

Answered or Unanswered? *by Louisa Vaughan* ISBN: *1-59462-248-5* **$10.95**
Miracles of Faith in China Religion Pages 112

The Edinburgh Lectures on Mental Science (1909) *by Thomas* ISBN: *1-59462-008-3* **$11.95**
This book contains the substance of a course of lectures recently given by the writer in the Queen Street Hall, Edinburgh. Its purpose is to indicate the Natural Principles governing the relation between Mental Action and Material Conditions... New Age/Psychology Pages 148

Ayesha *by H. Rider Haggard* ISBN: *1-59462-301-5* **$24.95**
Verily and indeed it is the unexpected that happens! Probably if there was one person upon the earth from whom the Editor of this, and of a certain previous history, did not expect to hear again... Classics Pages 380

Ayala's Angel *by Anthony Trollope* ISBN: *1-59462-352-X* **$29.95**
The two girls were both pretty, but Lucy who was twenty-one who supposed to be simple and comparatively unattractive, whereas Ayala was credited, as her Bombwhat romantic name might show, with poetic charm and a taste for romance. Ayala when her father died was nineteen... Fiction Pages 484

The American Commonwealth *by James Bryce* ISBN: *1-59462-286-8* **$34.45**
An interpretation of American democratic political theory. It examines political mechanics and society from the perspective of Scotsman James Bryce Politics Pages 572

Stories of the Pilgrims *by Margaret P. Pumphrey* ISBN: *1-59462-116-0* **$17.95**
This book explores pilgrims religious oppression in England as well as their escape to Holland and eventual crossing to America on the Mayflower, and their early days in New England... History Pages 268

QTY

The Fasting Cure *by Sinclair Upton*   ISBN: *1-59462-222-1* **$13.95**
In the Cosmopolitan Magazine for May, 1910, and in the Contemporary Review (London) for April, 1910, I published an article dealing with my experi-
ences in fasting. I have written a great many magazine articles, but never one which attracted so much attention... New Age/Self Help/Health Pages 164

Hebrew Astrology *by Sepharial*   ISBN: *1-59462-308-2* **$13.45**
In these days of advanced thinking it is a matter of common observation that we have left many of the old landmarks behind and that we are now pressing
forward to greater heights and to a wider horizon than that which represented the mind-content of our progenitors... Astrology Pages 144

Thought Vibration or The Law of Attraction in the Thought World   ISBN: *1-59462-127-6* **$12.95**
by William Walker Atkinson   Psychology/Religion Pages 144

Optimism *by Helen Keller*   ISBN: *1-59462-108-X* **$15.95**
Helen Keller was blind, deaf, and mute since 19 months old, yet famously learned how to overcome these handicaps, communicate with the world, and
spread her lectures promoting optimism. An inspiring read for everyone... Biographies/Inspirational Pages 84

Sara Crewe *by Frances Burnett*   ISBN: *1-59462-360-0* **$9.45**
In the first place, Miss Minchin lived in London. Her home was a large, dull, tall one, in a large, dull square, where all the houses were alike, and all the
sparrows were alike, and where all the door-knockers made the same heavy sound... Childrens/Classic Pages 88

The Autobiography of Benjamin Franklin *by Benjamin Franklin*   ISBN: *1-59462-135-7* **$24.95**
The Autobiography of Benjamin Franklin has probably been more extensively read than any other American historical work, and no other book of its kind
has had such ups and downs of fortune. Franklin lived for many years in England, where he was agent... Biographies/History Pages 332

Name	
Email	
Telephone	
Address	
City, State ZIP	

☐ **Credit Card**   ☐ **Check / Money Order**

Credit Card Number	
Expiration Date	
Signature	

Please Mail to: Book Jungle
PO Box 2226
Champaign, IL 61825
or Fax to: 630-214-0564

ORDERING INFORMATION

web*: www.bookjungle.com*
email*: sales@bookjungle.com*
fax*: 630-214-0564*
mail*: Book Jungle PO Box 2226 Champaign, IL 61825*
or PayPal *to sales@bookjungle.com*

Please contact us for bulk discounts

DIRECT-ORDER TERMS

**20% Discount if You Order
Two or More Books**
Free Domestic Shipping!
Accepted: Master Card, Visa,
Discover, American Express